Max
and the Rainbow Rain Hat

Gus Clarke

Andersen Press
London

Max was not a happy little bunny.
He never smiled. He had no reason to.

Because right above Max's head there was a big black rain cloud, all of his own. He didn't know why. But when Max went out, Max got wet.

And anyone that stopped to talk to Max got wet too, unless they stood a long way off. Then, of course, he couldn't hear them very well and they couldn't hear him. So Max didn't have any friends.

The plants and the flowers were pleased to see Max because they could have a drink from his rain cloud. But Max didn't want to stand around in the rain talking to the plants and the flowers. They didn't have much to say.

And all the while,
as Max got wetter
and wetter, Max got
sadder and sadder.

Then, one rainy day, Max had an idea.

He collected all the feathers he could find. And a few twigs. And a little bit of string. Then he went straight home and started work. He worked late into the night.

And when he had finished he had made himself the most beautiful multi-coloured rain hat. Max put it on his head and looked in the mirror.

He was so pleased he almost smiled.

The next day, Max went out wearing his new rain hat. Rat was the first to admire the hat. "Nice hat," said Rat.

"Pardon?" said Max. Rat came closer and stood under the brim of the hat, out of the rain. "Nice hat," he said. "It looks like a rainbow."

Badger was next. He had to bend down to get under the hat but at least he was in the dry.

One or two others came
up to admire the hat.
But there wasn't enough
room for anyone else under
the brim of the hat so they
soon went away.

That night, Max set to work on the hat again. He made it even wider and a little bit higher. Just a little bit higher than Badger.

The next morning, Max set off in his big new rainbow rain hat. This time lots more people were able to shelter under his hat and talk to him and each other.

They chatted and chattered. Not just about the hat, though they all thought it was a wonderful hat, but about all sorts of new and interesting things that Max had never been able to talk about with anyone before. Max started to feel a strange new feeling.

That night, Max set to work on the hat again. He made it wider and even taller so it could cover all his new friends and even have room for some more.

The next morning,
as he left home,
Max was aware
that something felt
different. But he
didn't know what.

Badger and Rat called to him when they saw him coming. Max stopped and smiled at them.

"Hello, Badger! Hello, Rat!" he said. "Isn't it a lovely day?"

"Hello, Max. It certainly is a lovely day," they said. "But Max, why are you wearing your rain hat today?"

Max looked up.
All he could see
was his hat.
He took it off
and looked again.

The rain cloud had gone!
Max smiled a great big smile.
He suddenly knew what that
strange new feeling was.
He was feeling happy.

Max still has his rainbow rain hat. And he still has days when he feels a little sad, but then we all do.
But he never needed to wear his rain hat again. Well . . .

. . . only in the rain.

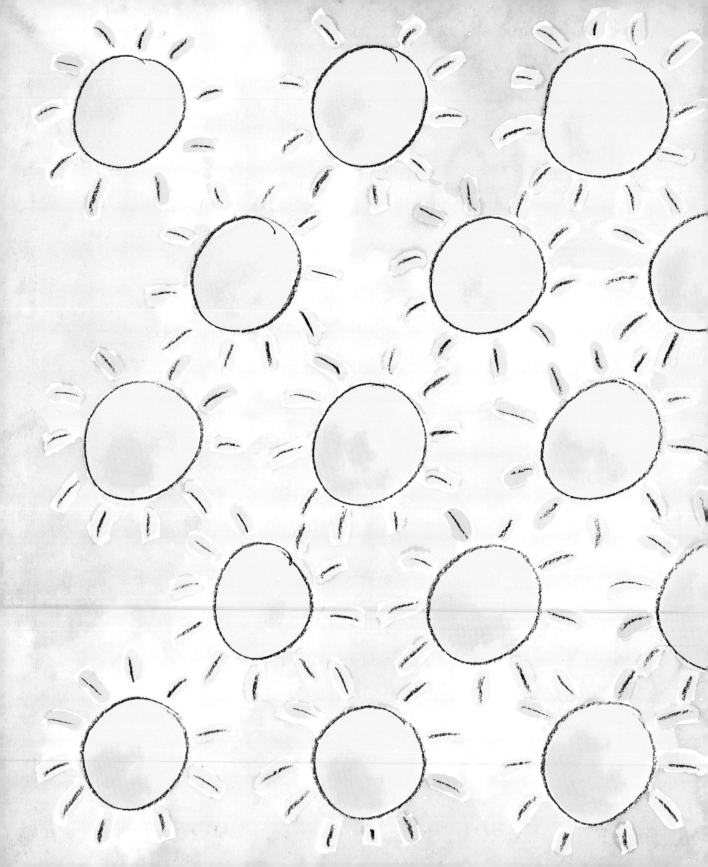